Olga's Dance

Written by Joe Hackett
Illustrated by Natalie Hinrichsen

WAYLAND

Olga was staying with Nana in the village. She was sitting at the kitchen table playing with her mobile phone.

"Olga, put away that silly phone and get some peppers from the cellar," said Nana.

"It's not silly!" said Olga, as she stomped down to the cellar.

It was the darkest place in Nana's house. Olga took a candle, found the peppers and ran back upstairs as fast as she could!

"Thank you," said Nana, as Olga gave her the peppers. "I'm making stuffed peppers for the village festival on Saturday. I dance every year!"

"It's only an old-fashioned village dance, Nana!" moaned Olga. "I don't want to go at all."

"Nonsense, you'll have great fun,"
said Nana.

Olga had stopped listening. She was
texting her friends in the city on her
mobile phone.

The next day, Nana and Olga went to get some pumpkins from Nana's field up on the mountain.

"What about the wolves that live on the mountain?" asked Olga, as they walked. "Is it safe?"

"We never see wolves any more,"
laughed Nana, "but be careful,
they're still up there!"

Olga was sure Nana was right but she was glad she had her mobile phone with her just in case.

Olga and Nana spent the afternoon collecting lots of pumpkins.

"Why do you need so many?" asked Olga, putting another pumpkin in the cart.

"To fatten up the pig," said Nana. "We must kill it before the snow comes so that we have plenty of meat this winter."

Olga was so upset at the thought of killing the pig that she didn't see Nana trying to carry an enormous pumpkin to the cart.

Suddenly Nana tripped over a rock sticking out of the ground. She dropped the pumpkin in surprise and fell down the steep hillside.

Olga ran as fast as she could, slipping and sliding everywhere.

"Nana, are you OK?" shouted Olga.

"Ouch, my leg!" said Nana. "Oh dear,
I don't think I can walk!"

Olga wasn't sure what to do! Just then she remembered her mobile phone and quickly rang her mum.

"Help, Mum. Nana's hurt herself
collecting pumpkins on the mountain!"
she cried.

"Don't worry, Olga," said her mum. "You
stay with Nana and I'll call the village
and get someone to send some help."

Nana and Olga had to wait so long it began to get dark. Olga was scared when she saw something coming. She thought it was a wolf!

Instead it was two men from the village. Olga's mum had told the men where to find Nana.

The men lifted Nana onto the back of the cart and they all went home.

The next day, Nana called Olga into her bedroom. She was sitting in bed, looking pale but smiling.

"Thank you for looking after me, Olga," said Nana.

"I'm glad you're OK, Nana," said Olga, giving Nana a hug.

"I'll soon be walking again but I won't be able to dance at the village festival tomorrow," said Nana sadly. "Would you dance for me, Olga?"

24

Just then Olga had a great idea.
"I will dance if you promise not to kill
the pig this year, Nana," she said.

"Deal!" laughed Nana, shaking
Olga's hand.

"You can wear the costume I used to wear as a girl," Nana cried. "It's in my wardrobe."

Olga got the dress and put it on.
It fitted perfectly!

At the village festival Olga joined in with
the dancing. It was a bit old-fashioned
but it was still good fun!

29

Back at home Nana and Olga had a hot drink before bedtime.

"You're right, Nana," said Olga. "Village customs aren't so bad after all!"

"And you're right, too," smiled Nana.
"Modern things can be useful. If it
wasn't for your mobile phone, we would
still be stuck up on that mountain!"

START READING is a series of highly enjoyable books for beginner readers. **The books have been carefully graded to match the Book Bands widely used in schools.** This enables readers to be sure they choose books that match their own reading ability.

Look out for the Band colour on the book in our Start Reading logo.

The Bands are:

Pink Band 1A & 1B

Red Band 2

Yellow Band 3

Blue Band 4

Green Band 5

Orange Band 6

Turquoise Band 7

Purple Band 8

Gold Band 9

START READING books can be read independently or shared with an adult. They promote the enjoyment of reading through satisfying stories, plays and non-fiction narratives, which are supported by fun illustrations and photographs.

Joe Hackett often visits a village in Bulgaria – one of his favourite countries –because the people are friendly and there's a lot of wildlife to see. He hasn't yet spotted a wolf but he knows they are up there in the forests and mountains somewhere!

Natalie Hinrichsen works in her loft studio in a suburb of Cape Town, South Africa. She has been illustrating children's books since 1996 and in 2005 she won the Vivian Wilkes award for illustration.